Here Comes
the Mystery Man

Here Comes the Mystery Man

BY SCOTT RUSSELL SANDERS
ILLUSTRATED BY HELEN COGANCHERRY

Bradbury Press   New York

Maxwell Macmillan Canada   Toronto
Maxwell Macmillan International
New York   Oxford   Singapore   Sydney

A Note from the Author

Brookville, the settlement in my story, is in southeastern Indiana. Although only a few days' walk from Cincinnati, in 1811 the village was so isolated that it might have been at the end of the earth. In October of that year, the first steamboat ever to travel down the Ohio River reached Cincinnati on its way to New Orleans. Steam-powered ships would soon connect the interior of America with the farthest seas, as peddlers' tales opened the minds of their listeners to the great and marvelous world.

———◆———

Bradbury Press
Macmillan Publishing Company
866 Third Avenue
New York, NY 10022

Maxwell Macmillan Canada, Inc.
1200 Eglinton Avenue East
Suite 200
Don Mills, Ontario M3C 3N1

Macmillan Publishing Company is part of the Maxwell Communication Group of Companies.

First edition
Printed and bound in Hong Kong by South China Printing Company (1988) Ltd.
10 9 8 7 6 5 4 3 2 1
The text of this book is set in 16 pt. Berkeley Oldstyle Medium.
The illustrations are rendered in watercolor.

LIBRARY OF CONGRESS CATALOGING-IN-PUBLICATION DATA
Sanders, Scott R. (Scott Russell), date.
Here comes the mystery man / by Scott Russell Sanders ;
illustrated by Helen Cogancherry.—1st ed.
p.   cm.
Summary: The Goodwin family's pioneer home is visited by the
traveling peddler, who brings wondrous things and amazing tales from
far away.
ISBN 0-02-778145-3
[1. Peddlers and peddling—Fiction. 2. Frontier and pioneer life—
Fiction.] I. Cogancherry, Helen, ill. II Title.
PZ7.S19786Hf   1993
[E]—dc20   92-24572

For the Wicker family:
Roger, Lisa, Rachel, Jordan, and Meghan
—S. R. S.

For Herb,
who makes everything work
—H. C.

The minister brought the news one October day when he rode into Brookville for his monthly preaching. The minister told the blacksmith, who told his apprentice, who told the stable boy, who ran to tell his friends. Soon children were racing through the village and out through the woods, from cabin to cabin, shouting: "The peddler is coming! The peddler is coming!"

The peddler's visits were as dependable as those of the wild geese that honked across the sky in wavery Vs. Like the geese, he came every spring at plowing time and every fall at harvest. Now it was harvest time. Potatoes and onions were ready for digging. Wild grapes and crab apples were ready for picking. Milkweed tufts drifted through the air. The maples glowed so brightly, they seemed to be filled with red candles. And the peddler was coming, as regular as the moon!

When the hollering reached the Goodwin farm, everyone stopped work to listen. Mr. Goodwin quit chopping wood. Mrs. Goodwin quit slicing pumpkins. The four Goodwin children—Annie and Joseph, Meg and John—were putting up shocks of corn in the field. The stalks rustled in their hands, the children were so excited. The peddler from Cincinnati!

What stories would he tell? What jingles would he sing? What tunes would he play on his long silver flute? What marvels would he bring in his great bulgy pack?

He would have to pass right by their cabin on his way from the river to the village on the bluff. The children hurried to finish gathering the corn so they might go wait for him by the road.

Meg

Joseph

Annie

John

Thirsty and hot, they stopped by the well for a drink, each one sipping from the dipper. Then they dashed by the cabin, calling "All done!" to their parents, and ran to lean on the zigzag fence by the road. It was a good strong fence, made from rails their father had split. Their log cabin was tight and warm. The dirt in their fields was rich and black. Nobody had the fevers or shakes. What else could a family want, besides a visit from the mystery man?

"What do you suppose he'll bring this time?" asked John.

"Maybe one of those umbrellas," Meg suggested.

"Or a magnifying glass," said Joseph.

"Or a chunk of fox fire that shines in the dark," said Annie.

The afternoon stretched on, the sun sank low. Their mother called them in for a supper of corn bread, turkey, beans, and pumpkin pie. Then evening chores—buckets of water to carry, dishes to wash, wood to fetch, hogs to feed—and still no peddler.

Their father called the children in for bed. But who could go to sleep? They diddled and dawdled. Again their father called.

"You want me to jerk a knot in your tails?"

Just then the children heard a whistle down by the river. It wasn't any bird, wasn't any beast. What else could it be but a flute? Then they heard a clink and a clank, like banging pots, and they knew for sure.

Clip and clop, here came the peddler, riding one horse and leading another. He wore a tall beaver hat with a feather in the band. His beard was black as charcoal and bushy enough to stuff a pillow. His belly was as round as a haystack.

The children gave a shout, and their parents came out of the cabin with a lantern. The family stood hushed by the road in a circle of light.

The peddler showed his silver teeth in a grin. "Unless I'm hoodwinked, it's the family Goodwinks."

"Right you are, Merchant Meeks," said Mrs. Goodwin.

"But who are all these big children?" the peddler asked. "They can't be the little ones I left in spring?"

"The very same," Mr. Goodwin said. "Sprouted up like corn."

"You must be weary from the road," said Mrs. Goodwin.

"Won't you come eat a bit and spend the night?"

Now the children piped up. "Yes, do, please do!"

The mystery man removed his tall hat and laid it against his heart. "I can't think of a place on earth I'd rather stay."

They all helped unload the packs, which rattled and rang. The children brushed the sweaty horses and fed them hay.

Inside by the fire, the children watched the peddler eat. He was a small man, a bit taller than Joseph, but there was nothing small about his appetite. "Don't mind if I do," he replied, every time Mrs. Goodwin offered him a dish. He finished the corn bread, the turkey, the beans. He was on the last slice of pumpkin pie when he leaned back, patted his belly, and sighed. "A feast for a king, Mrs. Goodwin, a feast for a king."

The children kept quiet as rabbits, not wishing to be sent off to bed. But finally John could stand it no longer, and he whispered, "What did you bring? What stories? What things?"

The peddler plucked his beard. "I might have a surprise or three." He unbuckled a pouch and drew from it a glass bottle. This he handed to John, saying, "What do you see inside?"

"A teeny tiny ship!" cried John. "How did it get in there?"

"Must have got lost in a storm," said the peddler.

Then, item by item, he spread his goods upon the hearth. Tea from China, ink from India, calico cloth from England, an ivory comb from Africa, a razor from Spain, seeds from the Shakers in Kentucky. The world is so big! thought the children. The peddler brought out flints for muskets, beeswax for candles, buttons of brass and pewter and horn. There was a looking glass, a silk shawl, linen thread and iron nails, scissors, tweezers, clay pipes, cigars, a jar of elixir, and a tin cup to drink it from. When he brought out spices, the cabin filled with the smell of cinnamon.

After considering their needs and counting out their coins, Mr. and Mrs. Goodwin bought a basket, a length of cloth, some harness buckles, fishhooks, two iron forks, a brass pen for writing letters, and a silver thimble for sewing. The children studied these new possessions and handled them carefully.

"Try these," the peddler said, offering the children a pair of shiny spectacles with square lenses in wire frames.

They took turns gazing through the spectacles, which made everything in the cabin seem bulgy and blurry, the way a catfish looks underwater in the creek.

"And take a peep at this," said the mystery man. The children crowded near. In his cupped hand they saw a shiny brass disk with a window on the top, and inside, a little arrow that spun round and round on a pin. "Whatever is it?" Meg asked.

"It's called a compass," the peddler answered.

"What's the arrow doing?" John asked.

"Sniffing around to find which way is north. Just watch." The arrow seesawed for a moment, then settled down and pointed straight through the fire toward the back of the chimney. The children looked up at their father, who always knew directions from the sun and stars.

"That's north, sure enough," said Mr. Goodwin.

The children whistled. The mystery man reached again into his pouch. What he cupped in his hand this time looked like a peeled potato, smooth and creamy, one end flat and the other pointy. "Go ahead and touch," he said. It felt hard and cool. The children called out their guesses: Was it a turnip? A knot of wood? A buffalo horn? A stone? Cane sugar? Ice?

The peddler's laugh made his black beard wag and his silver teeth wink. "My dears," he said, "it's the tooth of a whale."

A whale? From the deep blue sea? Yes, indeed, he told them. A whale bigger than their cabin, bigger than the trading post in Brookville, a creature that dived to the bottom of the ocean and rose back up to huff and puff. It could leap clear out of the water and come splashing down with a sound like thunder, could swallow a wagonload of fish at one gulp, could swim all the way around the earth.

Listening to him, the children felt tingly. Such a huge world, and so full of wonders!

"And do you know," said the peddler, "just the other day in Cincinnati I saw a fine thing—a boat that runs on fire. They burn wood in a stove to heat water, the water makes steam, the steam drives a piston, the piston turns gears, the gears turn paddle wheels, and the paddles drive the boat through the water. A steamboat, they call it."

Watching the flames in their fireplace, the children could picture such a boat, but they could hardly believe it possible.

"Just imagine," said the peddler, "on a steamboat you could sail down the Ohio River to the Mississippi, down the Mississippi to the Gulf of Mexico, then far into the ocean on the lookout for whales, and you'd never get lost so long as you carried your compass." Just imagine! thought the children.

"It's about time four young ones carried themselves off to sleep," said Mrs. Goodwin.

"May I give them a little present first?" asked the peddler.

"If they promise to skedaddle into bed," said their mother.

The children promised. Then, into each child's hand the mystery man placed a chunk of maple sugar. They all said thank you before licking the candy. It was so good, so sweet!

Quickly they washed their faces in the bucket by the fire, kissed their mother, kissed their father, climbed up the ladder to the loft, slithered into their nightshirts, then snuggled under the quilt. The corn husks in the pallet rustled beneath them. "Good-night!" they called.

"Sleep well," said their father.

"Sweet dreams," said their mother.

"See you in the spring," said the mystery man.

The children knew he would leave before dawn. If only they could travel with him for a time! But there would be chores to do in the morning—fish to catch, grapes to gather, hogs to chase in the woods. So Annie and Joseph, Meg and John lay there thinking of spring, with the taste of maple sugar on their tongues. As they drifted off to sleep, they imagined steamboats and whales, rivers and distant lands. The last sounds they heard were the snapping of the fire, the tootle of a flute, and, from high in the sky, the honking of geese.